Lucky bat lost?

"Does anyone want to com[...]
We have those really awe[...]
with vanilla ice cream in the middle."

"Yum!" Bess said enthusiastically. She glanced under one of the benches in the dugout. "I'll be ready in a second, as soon as . . . hey, have you guys seen Magic Bill?"

Nancy frowned. "No."

"Where did you leave it?" George asked Bess.

"I *thought* I left it right here," Bess said, sounding worried.

"Let's look around," Nancy suggested.

Nancy, Bess, and George searched all over the dugout. Then they went outside and searched all around the field. But there was no sign of Bess's bat.

Bess turned to Nancy and George. She looked as though she was about to burst into tears. "Magic Bill is missing!" she cried out.

The Nancy Drew Notebooks

Available from Simon & Schuster

THE
NANCY DREW
NOTEBOOKS®

#65

Strike-Out Scare

CAROLYN KEENE
ILLUSTRATED BY JAN NAIMO JONES

Aladdin Paperbacks
New York   London   Toronto   Sydney

This book is a work of fiction. Any references to historical events, real people, or real locales are used fictitiously. Other names, characters, places, and incidents are the product of the author's imagination, and any resemblance to actual events or locales or persons, living or dead, is entirely coincidental.

❦ ALADDIN PAPERBACKS
An imprint of Simon & Schuster Children's Publishing Division
1230 Avenue of the Americas, New York, NY 10020
Copyright © 2005 by Simon & Schuster, Inc.
All rights reserved, including the right of reproduction in whole or in part in any form.
ALADDIN PAPERBACKS, NANCY DREW, THE NANCY DREW NOTEBOOKS, and colophon are registered trademarks of Simon & Schuster, Inc.
Designed by Lisa Vega
The text of this book was set in Excelsior.
Manufactured in the United States of America
First Aladdin Paperbacks edition March 2005
10 9 8 7 6 5 4 3 2 1
Library of Congress Control Number 2004116508
ISBN 1-4169-0073-X

Strike-Out Scare

1

Magic Bill

P lay ball!" eight-year-old Nancy Drew exclaimed. She punched her fist into her leather baseball glove as she skipped down the sidewalk.

"Batter up!" her friend George Fayne said, skipping next to her.

"Three strikes and you're out!" George's cousin Bess Marvin yelled, swinging a sky blue bat at her side. "Or is it four?"

Nancy giggled. Bess was not exactly a big sports fan. On the other hand, George loved just about every sport on the planet, especially baseball.

It was a beautiful spring day. The three girls had just started their spring vacation. They were on their way to the park for their first day of baseball practice. They had signed up to play for the Mahoney Marlins. Nancy was going to be a pitcher. George was going to be a shortstop. Bess was going to be a catcher.

Nancy and George had to talk Bess into playing for the Marlins. Luckily, Bess finally agreed. She didn't want to miss a chance to hang out with her two best friends—even if it *was* on a baseball field!

The three friends soon reached the park. Nancy noticed a bunch of girls about their age doing stretches on the baseball diamond.

"There's our team," Nancy said excitedly. "Come on!"

Nancy, George, and Bess ran across the park. A tall, athletic-looking woman in a blue and yellow T-shirt waved them over. It was their coach, Coach Gloria. Nancy remembered her from sign-up day the week before.

"Good morning, girls!" Coach Gloria called

out cheerfully. "Ready to play some ball?"

"Yes!" Nancy, George, and Bess said in unison.

Coach Gloria smiled at them. She had long black hair that she wore in a ponytail. Her blue and yellow baseball cap had the letter *M* on it and matched her T-shirt and shorts. She wore a silver whistle on a string around her neck.

"Let me show you where you can put your things," Coach Gloria offered. She pointed to Bess's blue bat. "You brought your own bat? That's awesome! You must be a serious hitter."

"My mom and dad bought it for me yesterday as a special present," Bess explained. "Isn't it beautiful? I'm only an okay hitter, though. Nancy and George and I play with some kids from school sometimes. I fly away a lot."

"Fly *out*," George whispered, correcting her.

A young boy with brown hair and glasses came up to them. He was carrying an armful of bats.

"Where do I put these, Mom?" he asked Coach Gloria in a grumpy-sounding voice. "They're heavy!"

"Just put them over in the dugout, Austin," Coach Gloria told him. "Girls, this is my son Austin. He's my assistant. Austin, this is Nancy, Bess, and George. George, do you prefer George or Georgia?"

"George, definitely," George said quickly.

"We're starting batting practice in a few minutes," Coach Gloria said. "Why don't you get settled in and do some stretches with the others?"

"Okay," Nancy said, nodding.

Nancy and her friends put their gloves on a bench in the dugout. Bess put her bat there too. Then the three of them rushed out to the field to join the other girls.

"Hey," one of the girls said to Nancy. "Are you a pitcher?" The girl had long, wavy brown hair and dark brown eyes. She spoke with a slight accent.

Nancy was surprised. "Yes! How did you know?"

The girl giggled. "I played baseball in Caracas. You look like a pitcher!"

"Caracas, where's that?" George asked the girl curiously.

"It's the capital of Venezuela, in South America," the girl replied. "I'm Rita Valero."

Nancy, George, and Bess introduced themselves. "I didn't know they played baseball in South America," Bess said. "That's so cool!"

Rita nodded. "South Americans *love* baseball! I played all the time there, before my family moved to River Heights. I played something called *chapitas,* too. That's like baseball, except you hit with broomsticks and bottle caps instead of bats and balls."

"That sounds like fun!" Nancy said eagerly.

"I have a bottle cap collection in a shoe box," George said. "Maybe we can play *chapitas* with them sometime."

Just then Coach Gloria blew her whistle. "Okay, everyone, listen up!" she said loudly. "We're going to start today with some batting practice. I want you to line up over there." She pointed to a spot about ten feet to the left of home plate. "I'll pitch. We'll rotate catchers. Rita, why don't you catch first?"

"Sure, Coach Gloria!" Rita replied.

Bess went to the dugout to get her blue bat. Then she, Nancy, and George joined the other girls in line.

"What kind of bat is *that*?" one of the girls asked Bess. She had short honey-blond hair and lots of freckles sprinkled across her cheeks.

"It's my new bat," Bess explained to the girl. "I really love it!"

"I've never seen a bat that color," the girl said. "It's pretty cool."

"Thanks," Bess said.

"Charlotte Karol, you're up!" Coach Gloria called out.

The girl with the honey-blond hair turned around. "Okay, Coach!"

Charlotte strolled up to the plate. Austin handed her a silver-colored bat.

"Go, Charlotte!" a woman in the bleachers called out. "You can do it, honey!"

Nancy glanced over at the woman. She had the same honey-blond hair as Charlotte. She must be Charlotte's mom, Nancy guessed.

Charlotte clenched her bat with both hands and fixed her eyes on the ball in

Coach Gloria's glove. She had a fierce expression on her face. She seemed to be concentrating very hard.

Coach Gloria threw the pitch. Charlotte's bat made a loud noise as it struck the ball. The ball went flying into left field.

Charlotte's mother jumped to her feet. "Yay, Charlotte! Way to go, sweetheart!" she yelled.

Charlotte turned beet red. She looked embarrassed by her mother's cheering.

"Nice contact, Charlotte!" Coach Gloria praised her. "Bess Marvin, you're up next."

"Oh, boy," Bess whispered anxiously to Nancy and George. "I don't think I can do *that*."

"Just do the best you can," Nancy whispered back.

"Keep your eyes on the ball," George added.

"Maybe my new bat will give me luck," Bess said hopefully.

Bess walked up to the plate, looking nervous. She got into batting position and waited for the pitch.

Nancy crossed her fingers behind her

back. "Go, Bess!" she said under her breath.

Bess swung at the first pitch and missed. "Try again," Coach Gloria said to her encouragingly.

The second pitch came. Bess swung—and hit the ball!

Nancy and George both gasped. The ball arced high up in the air and landed in left field, almost at the fence. It had traveled even farther than Charlotte's ball.

"Yay, Bess!" Nancy cried out.

"Way to go, Marvin!" George said, clapping.

Bess turned around. She had a big smile on her face. "I can't believe I did that!" she cried out.

"I can see you're going to be one of our ace hitters, Bess," Coach Gloria said. She gave Bess a thumbs-up sign. "Good job. George Fayne, you're next!"

"Okay," George said, stepping up to the plate.

George got a short hit during her turn. Nancy did too. When Coach Gloria got to the end of the line, she had each of the girls bat a few more times.

When it was Bess's turn again, she hit a long line drive almost out to the right-field fence. A line drive is a hit that flies straight through the air rather than going up and coming back down again. On her third turn, Bess got another line drive, this time to center field.

Coach Gloria called a five-minute water break. Nancy and George rushed up to Bess. "When did you become such a totally awesome hitter?" George teased her cousin.

"I didn't," Bess replied. She held up her blue bat. "I think it's this bat. It must be a magic bat or something."

"There's no such thing as a magic bat, silly," Nancy said, giggling.

"Well, *this* one is. I'm going to start calling it 'Magic Bill,'" Bess said with a grin.

"If Magic Bill helps you hit like this all season, our team is definitely going to be number one!" George exclaimed.

Just then, an unfamiliar-sounding voice rang out. "In your dreams!"

2

Bess Makes a Bet

Nancy turned around. *Who was that?* she wondered.

A girl was standing on the other side of the fence behind home plate, near the bleachers. She was wearing a green T-shirt with a white letter *R* on it.

"She's a Raccoon," George whispered.

Bess frowned. "George! That's not a very nice thing to call someone."

"No, I mean she's a River City Raccoon. They're another baseball team in our league," George explained.

"Oh!" Bess said.

Nancy walked up to the girl. "Are you talking to us?" she asked curiously.

The girl nodded. "I'm Alana Antiles. You've probably heard of me, right?"

"Um, no, we've never heard of you," Bess said with a frown. "Why, are you famous or something?"

Alana tossed her long, pale blond hair over her shoulders. "I'm the star pitcher for the River City Raccoons," she said smugly. "We have a game with you guys on Friday. I just wanted to see if any of you knew how to hit."

"Why?" George asked her.

"So I can plan my pitching strategy. But I'm not worried. None of you know how to hit!" Alana said with a mean smile.

Bess put her hands on her hips. "What are you talking about?" she demanded. "All the Marlins know how to hit!"

"You wish. Magic bat or no magic bat, the Raccoons are going to cream the Marlins on Friday!" Alana announced.

"No way!" Bess said huffily.

"Oh, yeah?" Alana shot back.

"Yeah!" Bess glared at Alana. "Hey, I'll

make you a bet. The *Marlins* are going to cream the *Raccoons* on Friday."

Alana glared back. "Yeah? You're on! Loser has to buy the winner a pack of deluxe baseball cards."

"Fine!"

"Fine!"

The two girls shook on it. Nancy turned to George. "Now we *have* to win on Friday," she whispered.

George nodded. "Yeah. Otherwise, Bess has to buy Ms. Attitude a pack of baseball cards."

Nancy swung her legs back and forth, kicking up dust with her baseball cleats. It was Monday afternoon in the sixth and last inning of their very first game.

Unfortunately the Marlins were losing. Their opponents, the Skyville Sharks, were winning by a score of 7-5.

"Come on, Charlotte!" Nancy yelled loudly. Charlotte Karol was up at bat. There were two outs and no one on base.

"Go, Charlotte!" George yelled too. She leaned over to Nancy and Bess. "If we don't

get two runs this inning, we'll lose," she said worriedly.

Nancy nodded. "I know."

"I'm up after Charlotte and Rita," Bess said to Nancy and George. "I'm counting on Magic Bill to get me another hit!" She patted her blue baseball bat, which was lying across her lap.

"You've definitely had more hits today than anyone on the team," George said. "Maybe Magic Bill really *is* magic."

Just then Rita Valero came running up to Bess. "I'm up next!" she said breath-lessly. "Can I ask you a favor? Can I borrow your magic bat? I really need to get a hit here!"

Bess looked startled. "Uh . . . that is . . . well, I'd really like to. But my parents said I wasn't allowed to let anybody borrow it."

"Oh." Rita looked disappointed. "Okay."

Rita walked back to the on-deck circle to wait for her turn at bat. Bess watched her with a glum expression. "Now I feel bad. Maybe I should let her borrow it anyway!"

"If your parents said no, then you can't," George reminded her.

"I guess," Bess said.

15

Charlotte ended up getting a base on balls. That meant that the pitcher had thrown four pitches that were not in the strike zone. Charlotte was free to go to first base without getting a hit.

"You should have swung at that last pitch, honey!" Charlotte's mother called out from the bleachers. "You could have gotten a double, maybe a triple!"

Charlotte blushed and didn't look at her mother. Nancy felt sorry for Charlotte.

After Charlotte, Rita ended up getting a base on balls too. Now Charlotte was on second base, and Rita was on first base. There were two outs.

Coach Gloria came up to Bess. "No pressure, Bess," she said, patting her on the shoulder. "Just relax and do the best you can."

"Good luck, Bess," Nancy called after her.

"You can do it!" George cheered.

Bess walked up to the plate, wrapped her hands tightly around her bat, and held it up in the air. The pitcher for the Skyville Sharks was a red-haired girl named Alex. Alex threw a hard first pitch in Bess's direction.

Bess swung—and missed. "Strike one!" the umpire called out. The umpire is the person behind home plate who decides which pitches are strikes and which ones are not. He makes other decisions too, like whether or not a runner is out at a base.

Bess took a deep breath and held up her bat again. Alex threw the second pitch.

There was a sharp *zzzzzing* as Bess's bat met the ball. The ball flew, flew, flew up into the sky. Nancy, George, and everyone else on the Marlin team watched with bated breath as the ball curved over a grove of pine trees.

Seconds later the ball landed on the other side of the center-field fence. "Home run!" the umpire shouted.

"We won!" one of the Marlins cried out.

"We won!" the whole team cried out in unison.

Nancy and George jumped to their feet and gave each other a big hug. Then Nancy watched excitedly as Charlotte rounded the bases and touched home plate. She was followed by Rita, then Bess.

The whole team gathered around Bess

when she reached home plate. "Our hero!" one of the girls shouted.

"Home Run Bess!" another girl whooped. "That's what we're going to call you from now on."

Bess's face was glowing. She grinned at Nancy and George and said, "See? I *told* you Magic Bill was really magical!"

"I think *you're* the magical one," Nancy told her proudly. "You're an awesome hitter, Magic Bill or no Magic Bill!"

Everyone continued to give Bess hugs and pats on the back as the scoreboard lit up with the final score: MARLINS 8, SHARKS 7.

Just then Nancy noticed something out of the corner of her eye. Charlotte Karol was standing a little ways away from the crowd. She didn't look very happy.

"I think that's everything," Nancy said.

She stuffed her glove into her backpack and smiled at Bess and George. The rest of the Marlins had gone home. Nancy and her friends were the last to leave. Bess had wanted to linger after the game and practice catching and throwing.

"I'm ready," George said. She hoisted her backpack over her shoulders. "Does anyone want to come over to my house? We have those really awesome blue popsicles with vanilla ice cream in the middle."

"Yum!" Bess said enthusiastically. She glanced under one of the benches in the dugout. "I'll be ready in a second, as soon as . . . hey, have you guys seen Magic Bill?"

Nancy frowned. "No."

"Where did you leave it?" George asked Bess.

"I *thought* I left it right here," Bess said, sounding worried.

"Let's look around," Nancy suggested.

Nancy, Bess, and George searched all over the dugout. Then they went outside and searched all around the field. But there was no sign of Bess's bat.

Bess turned to Nancy and George. She looked as though she was about to burst into tears. "Magic Bill is missing!" she cried out.

3

Two Clues

Nancy couldn't believe it. How could Magic Bill be missing?

"Someone stole Magic Bill!" Bess moaned.

"Maybe there was a mix-up," Nancy said, trying to make Bess feel better. "Maybe somebody took Magic Bill home by mistake."

"How could anyone take Magic Bill by mistake? Everyone knows it's mine. It's the only blue bat!" Bess pointed out.

Nancy was silent. Bess was right. Still, it was hard to believe anyone would have taken Magic Bill on purpose.

Bess sat down on one of the benches and

covered her face with her hands. "My baseball career is doomed," she groaned. "I'm never going to get another hit as long as I live."

"Of course you will!" Nancy reassured her.

"Besides, we're going to find Magic Bill," George added.

Bess glanced up. "Do you think so? Do you think we can find Magic Bill?" she said hopefully.

Nancy nodded. "Definitely! Tomorrow at practice, I'm going to ask every single team member about Magic Bill. I bet someone knows where it is."

"Magic Bill?" Charlotte repeated. "No, I haven't seen Magic Bill. Why?"

It was Tuesday morning. Nancy, Bess, and George had all shown up a few minutes early for practice so they could ask around about Magic Bill.

They had talked to almost all of their teammates already. They had asked Coach Gloria and her son Austin, too. So far no one knew anything about Magic Bill.

"Never mind," Bess said glumly to Charlotte. "Just let me know if you see it, okay?"

"Is Magic Bill missing?" Charlotte asked her.

Was Nancy imagining it, or did Charlotte sound kind of happy about it?

I must be imagining it, Nancy thought.

"There's Rita," Nancy said out loud to Bess and George. "Let's go talk to her!"

Nancy and her friends said good-bye to Charlotte and ran across the field. Rita was doing some stretches under a big oak tree.

"Hi, Rita!" Nancy called out.

Rita glanced up and smiled. "Hey, *amigas*! Did you bring your old bottle caps, George? Ready to play some *chapitas*?" she said cheerfully.

"Maybe another time," George replied. "Did you happen to take a bat home last night?"

Rita frowned. "A bat? You mean a baseball bat? No, why would I?"

"We were just wondering if anyone might have taken Magic Bill home by mistake," Nancy explained.

"Magic Bill?" Rita said curiously. "You mean your super-special bat, Bess? No, I definitely did not take it home with me." She paused and added, "Why? Did you lose it?"

"Maybe. We're not sure yet," Nancy said quickly. "Thanks a lot, Rita! Let us know if you see it, okay?"

"Of course!" Rita promised.

As they left Rita, Bess grabbed Nancy's arm. "No one knows anything about Magic Bill," she whispered. "That means it's definitely, one hundred percent, absolutely gone!"

Nancy nodded slowly. She had to agree. Magic Bill was gone. And most likely, someone had taken it—on purpose.

"Well, Magic Bill may *seem* like magic, but it didn't disappear into thin air," Nancy pointed out. "If someone took it, then there might be some clues."

Nancy got down on her knees and peered behind one of the benches in the dugout. It was really yucky under there. She saw lots of dirt and cobwebs. She noticed bubble gum wrappers and an old baseball cleat, too.

But there was no Magic Bill.

In the distance she heard Coach Gloria's voice: "Okay, I want everyone to run two laps around the field!"

Nancy stood up and brushed the dirt off her hands. She had sneaked away from practice for a few minutes to search the dugout for clues to Magic Bill's thief—if there *was* a thief. But so far she had turned up nothing.

I'd better get back to practice before Coach Gloria gets mad, Nancy thought as she walked toward the bleachers.

Just then she noticed something shiny wedged in a slot in one of the floorboards. She bent down and peered into the crack. There was definitely something there.

However, it was really stuck. Nancy couldn't pry it loose with her fingers.

Thinking quickly, she pulled one of her barrettes out of her hair. *This should work,* she told herself.

She poked at the shiny object with her barrette. After a few seconds it came loose.

Nancy picked it up and studied it. It was a coin.

But it wasn't like any coin she had ever

seen. It had a picture of a strange-looking duck on it. Above the duck, it said: CANADA. Below the duck was printed: DOLLAR.

"Canadian money!" Nancy said out loud.

She was about to get up when she saw something else—something she hadn't noticed before.

Deep in the shadows under one of the benches was a long, jagged piece of wood.

Nancy reached under the bench and pulled the wood out very carefully. She gasped when she realized what it was.

It was a piece of a broken baseball bat. The bat was made of light-brown wood. There were some words written on it in green marker.

The words said: MAGIC BILL.

4

A Raccoon Encounter

Nancy felt a shiver go down her spine. Someone had left a broken bat in the dugout with the words MAGIC BILL on it. *Creepy,* she thought.

Nancy turned the broken bat over in her hand. It was definitely not Magic Bill. Magic Bill was not made of wood.

Then she studied the words on the bat. The marker was not light green and not dark green but somewhere in between. She held it up to the sunlight. She saw that the ink had bits of glitter in it too.

This bat was definitely not here yesterday, Nancy thought. She and Bess and George had searched the dugout inside out. This meant that someone had left it here between yesterday and today.

Nancy wasn't sure about the Canadian coin. But she didn't think it was here yesterday either.

Nancy thought hard. There was only one reason someone would have left this broken bat here: to spook Bess about Magic Bill. And maybe that person dropped the Canadian coin by accident while he or she was planting the broken bat, she guessed.

"What are you doing?"

Nancy glanced up, startled. Coach Gloria's son Austin was standing in the doorway. He was wearing a blue and yellow Marlins baseball cap backward on his head.

Austin stared at the broken bat in her hand. "What're you doing with a wooden bat?" he asked her. "You're not allowed to have those."

"What do you mean?" Nancy asked him.

"You're not allowed to have wooden bats in the River Heights Junior Baseball League," Austin explained. "That's rule number 5.2 on page fifteen of the rule book," he rattled off.

"Wow, you really know the rules," Nancy said, impressed. "It's not my bat," she continued. "I found it under the bench. Do you know where it might have come from?"

Austin shook his head so hard that it made his glasses slide down his nose. "No way," he said. He glanced over his shoulder. "I'd better get back on the field before Mom gets mad."

"Yeah, me, too," Nancy said. She wrapped the broken bat carefully in one of her sweatshirts, then quickly put it and the Canadian coin into her backpack.

As she walked back onto the field, her mind was racing. Someone took Magic Bill after yesterday's game against the Skyville Sharks. Nancy was sure that the same person planted the broken bat sometime between then and now. That person had probably done it to make Bess think that Magic Bill was lying broken and useless somewhere.

What a mean, awful thing to do! Nancy thought. She felt sorry for Bess—and more determined than ever to find Magic Bill's thief.

"If the thief does anything to hurt Magic Bill, I will be really, really mad!" Bess exclaimed. She took a spoon and stuck it into her hot fudge sundae, making the whipped cream spill over the sides.

Bess, Nancy, and George were sitting in a booth at the Double Dip. The Double Dip was their favorite ice cream parlor. They had gone there for an after-lunch snack.

Nancy had told Bess and George all about the broken bat—and the Canadian coin, too. Seeing the broken bat with the words MAGIC BILL on it had made Bess more upset than ever.

"We *have* to find Magic Bill," Bess told Nancy. "I didn't get one hit at practice today!"

"That has nothing to do with Magic Bill," Nancy said. "You're just feeling bad."

"You don't understand, Nancy. I can't hit without Magic Bill!" Bess insisted. She plopped a big strawberry into her mouth and frowned.

George took a bite of her Super-Duper

Bubblegum Sundae. "We need to make a list of suspects," she suggested.

Nancy nodded. "Good idea. As soon as I get home, I'm going to get out my special blue detective notebook so we can—"

But Nancy was interrupted by the sound of a loud voice coming from another booth.

"The Raccoons are going to beat the Marlins on Friday," said the voice. "I made sure of it!"

5

Striking Out

Nancy whirled around in her chair. Someone was bragging that the Raccoons would beat the Marlins on Friday. That someone had a familiar-sounding voice. . . .

Nancy recognized the person right away. "Alana," she said under her breath.

Bess and George craned their necks. "What's *she* doing here?" Bess whispered.

Alana Antiles was sitting two booths away. She was with three other girls. They were all wearing the same green jerseys with the white letter *R* on them. The four Raccoons were sharing a huge banana split with lots of cherries on top.

Nancy frowned. *What did Alana mean? How did she make sure the Raccoons would beat the Marlins on Friday?* she wondered.

And then it occurred to her. Alana had made a bet with Bess that the Raccoons would beat the Marlins. Alana had been at the game yesterday when Magic Bill had disappeared. And now Alana was bragging to her teammates that she could guarantee the Raccoons' victory.

Nancy turned around. "I think Alana could be our thief," she whispered to her friends.

"What?" Bess and George burst out in unison.

Nancy put her finger to her lips. "Shhhhh! She'll hear us."

George leaned across the table. "Why do you think Alana is our thief?" she whispered.

Nancy explained her theory to George and Bess. When she was done, Bess looked even madder than before.

"You're right, Nancy. She *has* to be the thief!" she whispered angrily. "I'm going to go over there and make her give Magic Bill back right this second!"

Nancy put her hand on Bess's arm. "Wait. Let me talk to her, okay?" she suggested.

Bess nodded. "Okay. You're the detective."

Nancy got up and walked over to Alana's booth. Bess and George followed.

Alana looked up at Nancy and her friends. "Hey, Marlins!" she greeted them. "Have you come to beg for mercy?"

"Hi, Alana," Nancy said. "We have something to ask you."

"I know! You want to back out on our bet," Alana said to Bess. She turned to her teammates and cracked up.

Bess put her hands on her hips. "No way!"

"Well, that's too bad, because the Marlins are going to lose, lose, lose," Alana said meanly.

"What makes you so sure?" Nancy asked.

Alana shrugged. "I have a super-secret strategy."

"Like stealing Bess's bat?" Nancy blurted out.

Alana made a face. "What are you talking

about? Why would I want to steal Bess's stupid old bat?"

"It is *not* a stupid old bat!" Bess exclaimed. "It's magic!"

"Yeah, Alana!" George piped up. "You stole it because you were worried that Bess was going to hit a bunch of home runs on Friday."

Alana burst into laughter. "Are you kidding? Bess isn't going to hit a single home run off of me on Friday—magic bat or no magic bat!"

Nancy stared at Alana. "So what did you mean when you said you made sure the Raccoons would beat the Marlins?" she asked her.

"I meant . . . hey, I don't have to tell you!" Alana said, catching herself. "My super-duper winning strategy is top secret." She narrowed her eyes at Nancy. "You were eavesdropping on us, weren't you?"

Nancy shook her head. "No way. But you were talking in kind of a loud voice."

"I think you were eavesdropping," Alana accused her. "You're nothing but Marlin spies! And there's no way I'm going to tell you anything else about my top secret strategy!"

"Strike two!" the umpire exclaimed.

Bess wiped her forehead with the back of her hand as the pitcher stepped off the mound. Nancy watched her friend from the dugout and sighed. Bess was having another bad day at bat.

The Mahoney Marlins were playing a game against the Clifton Park Cougars. It was the fifth inning, with no outs. Rita was on first base. The Cougars were leading 4-2.

Bess had been up to bat twice today— and each of those times she had struck out. She just couldn't seem to make contact with the ball.

Nancy knew that Bess's hitting slump had nothing to do with the fact that she wasn't batting with Magic Bill. The problem was, Bess didn't know that. Bess really and truly believed that the only way she could get a hit was with Magic Bill.

George leaned over to Nancy. "We *have* to find Magic Bill before Friday," she whispered.

Nancy nodded. Friday was the big game against the Raccoons. "That's only two days away," she pointed out.

"I know," George said gloomily.

The pitcher threw the next pitch. Nancy and George held their breaths.

Bess swung—and missed. "Strike three!" the umpire declared.

Bess walked back to the dugout with a long face. Coach Gloria patted her on the shoulder. "Don't worry about it, Bess," she reassured her.

"Thanks, Coach Gloria," Bess said. She sounded really bummed out.

Bess plopped down next to Nancy and George. "I should probably just quit the team," she grumbled. "I'm totally useless!"

Nancy shook her head. "No way! First of all, you're an awesome catcher, and I need you. The *team* needs you. Second of all, you're just having a bad hitting streak."

"Bad? It's more like the worst hitting streak ever in baseball history," Bess corrected her.

George gave Bess a hug. "Don't worry, we'll find Magic Bill soon," she promised.

"At least *she's* getting lots of hits," Bess said, nodding in the direction of home plate.

Nancy glanced up. Charlotte Karol was up at bat. Bess was right. Charlotte had already gotten two hits today.

Then Nancy's eyes fell on something in the corner of the dugout. It was a big, dark green duffel bag with the initials CK on it in light green.

CK must stand for Charlotte Karol, Nancy thought.

Nancy could see the outline of something long and skinny bulging against the side of the bag.

It looked like . . . a bat.

Could it be Magic Bill? Nancy wondered.

6

Lost and Found?

Nancy frowned as she stared at Charlotte's bag. Could Charlotte have stolen Magic Bill?

Charlotte didn't look very happy the other day when the Marlins beat the Skyville Sharks. Bess had hit a home run in the last inning. Kids on the team had started calling her "Home Run Bess."

Until Magic Bill was stolen, Bess was the number one hitter on the team. Charlotte was number two.

Maybe Charlotte would have preferred to be number one, Nancy thought. Maybe she would have preferred to be "Home Run Charlotte."

Maybe she had taken Magic Bill to make sure of that.

"George! Bess!" Nancy whispered. "Take a look at that bag over there."

George and Bess followed Nancy's glance. "What is it, Nancy?" George whispered.

"It's Charlotte's bag," Nancy replied. "Doesn't that look like a bat inside of it?"

"I guess so," Bess said after a moment. Then she put her hands on her mouth and gasped. "You don't think it's Magic Bill, do you?"

"I don't know," Nancy said. "But I'm going to find out."

Nancy glanced over at home plate. Charlotte was still up at bat.

"Stay here," Nancy told her friends.

Nancy got up from her seat on the bench and walked over to the corner. She sat down on that end of the bench and pretended to do some leg stretches.

As she stretched, she leaned over and tried to peek inside Charlotte's bag. It was halfway open. But all Nancy could see was a rumpled green sweatshirt and a water bottle. She couldn't make out what the long, skinny object was.

"What are you doing?"

Nancy's head shot up. Austin was standing there. He was holding a bucket full of balls.

Nancy smiled nervously at him. "I'm just stretching," she told him. "The bench was too crowded over there."

Austin pushed his glasses up his nose. "Did your friend ever find her bat?" he asked her.

"No, we haven't found it yet," Nancy replied. "But we will!"

Coach Gloria called over Austin, and he shuffled off. Nancy glanced at home plate. Charlotte was just about to swing at a pitch.

But at the last minute Charlotte held the bat across the front of her chest, instead of over her shoulder. She hit the pitch lightly— *thunk*! The ball bobbed and bounced toward third base.

"Run, Charlotte! Run, Rita!" Coach Gloria shouted.

Charlotte headed toward first base at full speed. Rita, who had been on first, headed toward second.

The third-base player for the Clifton Park Cougars scooped up the ball and threw it to first base. The first-base player caught it and touched the base with her foot. "Out!" the umpire called, pointing to Charlotte.

Charlotte turned around and trotted back to the dugout. Rita was safe on second base.

"Nice sacrifice bunt, Charlotte!" Coach Gloria called out.

Nancy remembered what a sacrifice bunt was. It meant that Charlotte had hit the ball lightly on purpose, with her bat held out in front of her. That way the person on first base could run to second base—even though it meant Charlotte would be thrown out.

Now Charlotte was almost at the dugout. Nancy had to think quickly. *I've got to get her to let me see inside her duffel bag,* she thought.

Then Nancy had a great idea. She reached behind her head and yanked her purple scrunchie out of her hair. She held it over the opening in Charlotte's bag and let go of it.

"What are you doing with my bag?"

It was Charlotte. She was walking into the dugout. She stared curiously at Nancy, then down at her bag.

"Hey, Charlotte," Nancy said, smiling. "Awesome bunt! Hey, this is your bag, right? I dropped my scrunchie into it by accident while I was doing some stretches. I'm really sorry, but could you get it for me?"

Charlotte looked confused. "Um, sure."

She sat down on the bench next to Nancy and leaned over to unzip her bag all the way. Nancy watched carefully as Charlotte dug through the contents in search of Nancy's scrunchie.

"What color is it?" Charlotte asked Nancy.

"Purple," Nancy replied.

Charlotte pulled her sweatshirt out of her bag and threw it on the bench. Just then Nancy caught sight of the long, skinny object. It didn't look quite like a bat. But she couldn't be sure. . . .

"What's that?" Nancy asked, pointing to the object.

Charlotte followed Nancy's glance. "Oh, this? It's . . . it's nothing."

"No, really, what is it?" Nancy persisted.

Charlotte blushed. She pulled the object out of the bag. It was a cardboard tube. Charlotte pulled a rolled-up poster out of it.

Nancy's heart sank. *So it isn't Magic Bill after all,* she thought.

"It's a poster of my favorite ballet dancer in the Chicago Ballet Company," Charlotte explained as she unrolled the poster. "I like dance way better than baseball. I only play baseball because . . . well, my mom really wants me to."

Nancy was surprised. "But you're so good at it!"

Charlotte shrugged. "Thanks. Baseball's okay. My mom wants me to play because she used to play when she was a kid. But if it was up to me, I'd take ballet lessons every day of the week!"

Nancy smiled at Charlotte. No wonder Charlotte sometimes seemed kind of unhappy.

Cross Charlotte off the suspect list, Nancy thought.

"Pass the popcorn, please," Bess said.

Nancy handed Bess the popcorn bowl.

Bess and George were at Nancy's house for a sleepover. Nancy loved sleepovers!

The Marlins had won their game against the Cougars that afternoon. Charlotte had gotten a home run in the last inning, making the final score 5-4.

Bess and George had come over to Nancy's house after the game. Now it was after dinner, and they were sitting on Nancy's bed. They had already changed into their pajamas. Nancy was wearing purple pajamas with pink polka dots. Bess was wearing white pajamas with bunnies. George was wearing red and blue striped pajamas.

Bess took a handful of popcorn and munched on it. "Mmm, yummy," she said.

"Hannah always puts just the right amount of butter on the popcorn," Nancy said. Hannah Gruen was the Drews' housekeeper. She had been with the family for the last five years, ever since Nancy's mother died.

George crossed her legs and turned to Nancy. "So! I guess Charlotte's not the bat thief," she said.

Nancy shook her head. "That means we have only one suspect left."

She reached over and pulled out a blue notebook from her desk. It was her special detective notebook. Her father had given it to her after she solved her first real case. Nancy used it for keeping track of suspects and clues.

Nancy opened the notebook to a clean page. She picked up her favorite purple pen and wrote:

SUSPECTS:

Alana. She and Bess have a bet about who's going to win the game on Friday. We heard her say that she has a plan for making sure the Raccoons win. She was at the game on Monday when Magic Bill disappeared.

CLUES:

1. A Canadian coin with a picture of a duck on it.
2. A broken wooden bat with the words MAGIC BILL on it. The words were written with a green marker with glitter in it.

Bess peered over Nancy's shoulder. "What about Rita?" she said suddenly.

"What *about* Rita?" Nancy asked her.

"She wanted to borrow Magic Bill from me, remember?" Bess answered. "I said no."

"But Rita is so *nice*," George said with a frown. "How could she be a thief?"

Bess shrugged. "I don't know. Maybe she really, really wanted Magic Bill and she didn't know how else to get it."

Nancy nodded. "You're right, Bess. We should at least put her on the suspect list." She added, "Maybe we should go to Rita's house tomorrow and talk to her."

"Good idea," Bess agreed.

Nancy walked up to the front door and rang the doorbell. "I hope Rita's home," she said to Bess and George.

It was Thursday morning. After a big breakfast of pancakes and strawberries, Nancy and her friends had gotten permission from their parents to walk around the corner to Rita's house.

"If Rita lives in our neighborhood, why

doesn't she go to our school?" George said.

"I think she goes to a private school," Nancy replied.

Just then the door opened. A tall, slender woman with short black hair was standing there.

She smiled at the girls. "Hello. Can I help you?" she said.

"Is Rita here?" Nancy asked. "We're friends of hers from the Mahoney Marlins."

"Oh, *si*, Rita's baseball team. Rita is playing in the backyard. You're welcome to go back there," the woman replied.

"Thank you!" Nancy, Bess, and George said all together.

The three girls walked down the driveway toward the backyard. Nancy thought the Valeros' house was pretty, with its pink shutters and window boxes full of red geraniums. There were lots of spring flowers in the garden, like daffodils and tulips.

Nancy and her friends turned the corner into the backyard. Suddenly, Bess stopped short and gasped.

Rita was sitting on the grass. There was a gray cat curled up next to her.

Rita was polishing a baseball bat with a cloth. The bat was sky blue.

It was Magic Bill!

7

The Big Game

Nancy couldn't believe her eyes. They had caught Rita with the evidence. There was no doubt about it. Rita was the thief!

Without waiting for Nancy and George, Bess ran up to Rita. Bess looked really mad.

"Give me back my bat!" Bess demanded.

Rita looked up, startled. "Hi, Bess. Hi, Nancy and George. You surprised me!"

"Why did you do it?" George asked Rita.

Rita frowned. "Why did I do what?"

"Why did you steal Magic Bill?" Nancy asked her.

"What are you talking about? I didn't steal Magic Bill," Rita said. Then she glanced at the bat in her hands. "Oh, you mean *this*. This isn't Magic Bill."

"Of course it is!" Bess insisted.

Rita shook her head. "No, it's not. It looks like Magic Bill, though. I saw it at a garage sale last night," she explained. "I asked my mom and dad if I could buy it with my allowance money. I wanted to clean it up and give it to you, Bess. As a present. I've been feeling really bad because you don't have your magic bat any more."

Nancy peered closely at Rita's bat. It was the same sky blue color as Magic Bill. But it was a slightly different shape. Plus, the handle part was different.

Bess also seemed to realize that this wasn't Magic Bill. She blushed deep red. "I'm really sorry I accused you, Rita," she apologized. "That was super-nice of you to get me a new bat."

"It's nothing," Rita said with a smile. "I know it's not the same as Bill. But maybe it will give you luck against the Raccoons tomorrow anyway."

Bess gave Rita a big hug. Rita hugged her back.

Nancy was relieved. She really liked Rita and was glad she wasn't the thief.

But that meant the thief was still out there somewhere—with Magic Bill.

And the big game against the Raccoons was tomorrow.

Nancy stood on the pitcher's mound and wound up for her pitch. She released the ball, aiming for Bess's mitt.

Alana swung at the pitch—and missed. "Strike three!" the umpire called.

Nancy took a deep breath. It was the second inning of the big Marlins-Raccoons game. The score was Marlins 0, Raccoons 0. Nancy had struck out three Raccoons hitters so far, including Alana.

But Alana, who was the pitcher for the Raccoons, had struck out *five* Marlins batters, including Nancy. Nancy had noticed that Alana had a really fast pitching style. She had never seen anything like it before.

Alana glared at Nancy and returned to the dugout. Bess lifted her catcher's mask from her face and grinned at Nancy. She mouthed the words, "Way to go, Nancy!"

Nancy smiled and mouthed, "Thanks!"

The next hitter grounded out to second base. That made it three outs, and it was the Marlins' turn at bat. Nancy, Bess, and the other Marlins on the field ran back to the dugout.

The people in the bleachers clapped and cheered. Nancy's dad, Carson Drew, was in the crowd. So was Hannah. Bess's parents and George's parents were sitting right behind them.

Mr. Drew waved at Nancy and gave her the thumbs-up sign. Nancy waved back.

"Rita, you're up," Coach Gloria called out as she looked over her clipboard. "George, you're after Rita, then Bess."

"I'm going to strike out," Bess complained to Nancy and George as she took off her catcher's gear.

"No, you won't," George reassured her. "You have a new magic bat."

"It's not a magic bat. It looks like Magic Bill, but it's not the same," Bess insisted.

Nancy put her hands on Bess's shoulders. "Bess. You're a great hitter, with or without Magic Bill. You just have to believe that, okay? We need you today. This is an important game."

Bess was silent for a moment. "Okay," she said finally. "I'll do my best." She added, "I still wish we could find Bill!"

"I know," Nancy said, nodding. "I'm going to keep looking for it, okay?"

"Okay," Bess said gratefully.

Nancy sat down in the dugout as George and Bess went to take some practice swings. Her mind was racing. Charlotte was not the thief. Rita was not the guilty one, either. Alana was the only suspect left.

Could it be her? Nancy wondered, watching Alana warming up on the pitcher's mound.

She tried to think of any clues she may have overlooked. Just then it came to her. The Canadian coin!

Nancy thought the thief might have dropped the coin when he or she planted the broken bat in the dugout. All Nancy had to do was find out who had dropped the coin.

She reached into her backpack and pulled out the coin. The second half of the inning had not yet started. She noticed that the umpire had called the two coaches over for a quick talk.

Nancy saw her chance and quickly ran up to Alana, who was at the pitcher's mound. Alana stared at her curiously. "What are you doing here?" she snapped.

Nancy showed her the coin. "I think you dropped this," she said.

Alana glanced at the coin. "That's not mine. What would I be doing with Spanish money, anyway?"

"Spanish? It's not Spanish, it's Canadian," Nancy corrected her.

"Whatever. It's not mine," Alana insisted.

She narrowed her eyes at Nancy. "I know what you're doing, Nancy Drew. You came out here to psych me out and mess up my pitching game. Well, you can just forget about that! I'm going to strike out every single Marlin until the game is over!"

"No way you're going to do that," Nancy said.

But she didn't want to argue with Alana any more. She had to keep looking for Magic Bill. She ran back to her team just as the game resumed.

Back at the dugout, Nancy started showing the Canadian coin to all her teammates. No one recognized it. No one even knew what it was.

Nancy was showing the coin to a girl named Susie when she was interrupted by a familiar voice.

"Hey, where'd you get that loonie?" the voice said.

8

An Unlikely Suspect

Nancy turned around at the sound of the voice. Austin was standing there.

"Loonie?" Nancy repeated, confused. "What's a loonie?"

"That's what Canadians call it," Austin explained. "It's because there's a picture of a loon on it."

"A loon?" Nancy repeated. "What's a loon?" She was beginning to feel silly asking all these questions.

Austin pointed to the bird on the coin. "That's a loon," he said patiently.

"Oh! I thought it was a duck," Nancy

said. She stared at Austin. "How do you know all this, anyway?"

"We're from Canada," Austin replied. "We moved here from Toronto when I was five."

"Oh," Nancy said.

And then something occurred to her. "Is this your loonie?" she asked Austin slowly. "I found it in the dugout a few days ago."

"Let me check the year," Austin said. He took the coin from her and peered closely at it.

Then he broke into a smile. "Yeah, it's mine! It's my lucky loonie. I was wondering where I lost it."

Nancy glanced at Austin's hands as he looked over his coin. He had drawn a smiley face on his right palm with a marker. Nancy looked again.

It was *green* marker. And the ink had specks of glitter that shimmered in the sunlight.

Nancy couldn't believe it. She had found her thief! "*You* stole Magic Bill," she burst out.

Austin's head shot up. His cheeks flushed. "W-what are you talking about?" he stammered.

"It had to be you," Nancy went on. "I found the broken bat on Tuesday, remember? You wrote the words MAGIC BILL on it in the same green marker you have on your hand. And I found this loonie—*your* loonie—near it."

Austin opened his mouth. Then he clamped it shut.

"Come on, just admit it," Nancy said.

Austin sighed. "Okay. I know what happened to Magic Bill. But I didn't *steal* it," he insisted.

Nancy frowned. "What do you mean?"

"I picked up all the bats and balls and stuff after Monday's game," Austin explained. "I picked up Magic Bill, too. I put everything in the dugout. Or I *thought* I did. But when I went back later, Magic Bill was the only bat missing."

"Do you think someone took it?" Nancy asked him.

Austin shook his head. "I don't know. I knew it was Bess's special bat so I put it behind the other bats. That way no one could see it. But I just can't figure out where it went."

Nancy thought for a moment. "Why did you leave the broken bat?" she asked him finally.

"I didn't want anyone to know I lost Magic Bill," Austin said miserably. "I was afraid my mom would be really mad. I found that broken wooden bat in the trash can. I figured if I wrote MAGIC BILL on it and left it in the dugout, everyone would think there was a thief."

"Oh," Nancy said.

"I made a big mistake, right?" Austin asked her sheepishly.

Nancy nodded. "Yeah. I think you should tell Bess and your mom everything. And then we need your help to find Magic Bill."

It was the bottom of the sixth and last inning. The Raccoons were winning 5-3.

It was Bess's turn at bat. Rita was on second base. George was on first base. There were two outs. If Bess got an out, that would be the end of the game.

"Come on, Bess!" Nancy shouted from the dugout.

"You can do it, Bess!" Charlotte joined in.

Bess stood at the plate, nervously clutching the bat that Rita had given her. So far she hadn't gotten any hits the entire game.

Nancy hadn't had any time to look for Magic Bill after she talked to Austin. But she knew Bess was an awesome hitter, with or without Magic Bill. She just hoped Bess knew it too, deep down.

Alana threw the first pitch. Bess swung at it—and missed.

"Strike one!" the umpire called out.

The second pitch was also a strike. Nancy gulped. *This isn't looking too good,* she thought.

Alana smiled a mean smile at Bess. "You ready to lose the bet?" she taunted.

"No way!" Bess yelled.

Alana got ready for the third pitch. She released the ball. It seemed to go a zillion miles a minute.

Nancy held her breath. *Come on, Bess,* she said to herself. *You can do it. I know you can. Just believe in yourself!*

Bess swung the bat. *Whack!*

Nancy jumped to her feet as Bess's bat made contact. The ball rose high up in the air. Dozens of heads looked up at the sky as everyone tried to follow its path.

The ball arced over the center-field fence and plopped down onto the soccer field next door. "It's a home run!" the umpire exclaimed.

Everyone began cheering and clapping wildly. The Marlins had won the game—thanks to Bess's home run!

Nancy and her teammates spilled out of the dugout as Rita, then George, then Bess ran to home plate.

Nancy was the first to reach Bess. "Yay!" she screamed, hugging Bess. "I knew you could do it!"

Bess's eyes were bright with excitement. "I couldn't let Alana win the bet," she said, giggling.

Rita gave Bess a hug too. "See, *chica*? The bat I gave you worked for you!"

Bess hugged Rita back. "Thanks, Rita! You're the best."

Just then Alana walked up to Bess. "Okay,

so I owe you a pack of deluxe baseball cards," she said. "Actually, you deserve it. That was a totally excellent hit."

Bess looked surprised. "Uh, thanks, Alana."

"I can't believe you hit a home run off one of my new fastball pitches," Alana said admiringly.

Nancy suddenly understood. "New fastball pitches? Alana, was that the super-duper, top secret strategy you were talking about at the Double Dip?"

Alana grinned. "Uh, *yeah*. What else did you think it was?" She turned to Bess. "Can you show me how you swing your bat sometime? If you do, I can show you some cool hitting tricks I know."

"Uh, sure," Bess said with a smile.

Coach Gloria came up to Bess. "Good job, Bess!" she praised her. "You really came through for us when we needed you."

Bess beamed. "Yeah! And I did it without Magic Bill. But I still really miss that bat," she added in a sad voice.

"I think that case is almost solved," Nancy told her.

Bess stared at her. "What are you talking

about, Nancy? Did you catch the thief?" she demanded.

"Not exactly," Nancy said mysteriously.

That night, Nancy got her notebook out of her desk. Then she curled up in her favorite comfy chair and began to write:

Today the Marlins beat the Raccoons 6–5. We almost lost. But Bess saved the day. She got a home run in the last inning! And she did it without Magic Bill!

She finally figured out that she's an awesome hitter with or without Magic Bill. She just had to believe in herself.

After the game, Austin told his mom that it was his fault Magic Bill was missing. He told her that he lost it while he was cleaning up the bats and balls after Monday's game. He apologized to his mom and to Bess.

I asked Austin a bunch of questions about Monday and made him retrace all his steps. It turned out that he had put all the bats in this one corner of the dugout.

I searched the corner more carefully. I found a big crack between the floor and the wall. Coach Gloria got a flashlight and we looked in the crack. Magic Bill had rolled down there by accident!

Austin crawled under the bench and got Magic Bill out. Bess was so happy! She even gave Austin a big hug and forgave him for everything.

She's going to start using Magic Bill again. But she's also going to use the bat Rita gave her. She named it Magic Belinda. But she knows now that feeling good about herself will help her hit better than any bat—magic or not.

Case closed!

THE
NANCY DREW
NOTEBOOKS®

Do you know a younger Nancy Drew fan?

Now there are mysteries just for them!

THIRD-GRADE DETECTIVES

Everyone in the third grade loves the new teacher, Mr. Merlin.
Mr. Merlin used to be a spy, and he knows all about secret codes and the strange and gross ways the police solve mysteries.

YOU CAN HELP DECODE THE CLUES AND SOLVE THE MYSTERY IN THESE OTHER STORIES ABOUT THE THIRD-GRADE DETECTIVES:

She's sharp.

She's smart.

She's confident.

She's unstoppable.

And she's on your trail.